Things

Alice Duer Miller

Alpha Editions

This edition published in 2023

ISBN : 9789357941082

Design and Setting By
Alpha Editions
www.alphaedis.com
Email - info@alphaedis.com

Contents

I

THE great alienist sat down at his desk, and having emptied his mind of all other impressions, held it up like a dipper for his new patient to fill. Large, blond, and handsome, she was plainly accustomed to being listened to. Before she had fairly undone her furs and folded her hands within her muff, the doctor's lateral vision had told him that, whatever her problems, it was not about her own nervous system that she had come to consult him.

Not too quickly her story began to take shape. Her household, her husband, her four children—three small boys and an older daughter, a girl of seventeen....

"My only thought has been my children, Dr. Despard."

"Your *only* thought, Mrs. Royce?"

She assented. The daughter was the problem—the daughter of seventeen.

"She and I have been such friends; I have always been a friend to my children, I hope, as well as a parent. And Celia's little arrangements, her clothes and her small parties, have been as much my interests as hers—more, perhaps. The bond between us has been peculiarly close until the last year or so. Lately a rebellious spirit has begun to develop. I have tried to make allowances, but naturally there are certain questions of manners and deportment—small but important—about which one cannot yield. I am almost ashamed to confess how unaffectionate are the terms that we have reached. The situation will strike you as a strange one between a mother and daughter——"

He shook his head. "You are by no means the only mother and daughter whose relations are unsatisfactory."

"Ah, the young people of to-day!" she sighed. "What *is* the matter with them, with the age, Dr. Despard? They are so hard, so individualistic. I myself was one of a large family, and we lived in the house with my grandparents and aunts. My life was made up of little duties for older people—duties I never thought of questioning. They were a pleasure to me. But if I ask Celia to go on an errand for me—or even to attend to something for herself—I am met by the look of a martyr or a rebel. But that is not the worst. At times, Dr. Despard, her language to me is violent—is—actually profane. I cannot help looking on this as an abnormal manifestation. At last I saw her case was pathological. No nice girl swears at her mother, and"—Mrs. Royce smiled—"my daughter is a nice girl."

It seemed to him that Mrs. Royce must be a very nice mother indeed. Soft, serious, and eminently maternal, she appealed profoundly to all his bachelor ideals.

"And your husband?" he asked. "How does he get on with his daughter?"

"Admirably," she returned warmly; "they hardly see each other."

He glanced quickly at her to see if her intention were humorous, but something mechanical in her smile had already warned him that her mind was bent on other of life's aspects than the comic. Now she was quite serious, and he replied with equal gravity:

"It is often the solution."

They decided, at length, that he was to spend a few days with them in the country. To bring the girl to his office would be useless. He would find her a gentle, well-behaved little creature, perhaps too much interested in her books. The exigencies of the children's education kept the Royces in town during the week, but they spent Saturday and Sunday at the old Royce place on the Hudson. Here Despard promised to come at the first opportunity.

She thanked him, and held out a strong, firm hand.

No, he thought when she had gone, he could not understand a girl's swearing at such a mother—at once so affectionate and so intelligent, for, with pardonable egotism, Despard reckoned her bringing the problem to him a proof of rare domestic intelligence. Most women would have made it the subject of anger or tears.

He himself held no special brief for youth. The younger generation did not attract him. His own nephews and nieces never made him return disgusted to his loneliness, but rather raised his enjoyment of his solitude.

Before he admitted his next patient he stood a moment contemplating the sacrifices made by a parent. "It's stupendous, it's too much," he thought; and smiled to think that, if he had married, a child of his might now be conducting him to a doctor's office, for of the two he would undoubtedly have been the first to swear.

After a week particularly crowded with the concerns of other people Despard arrived, at high noon of a day in early April, at the Royces' place. Never, he thought, had he seen peace so clearly embodied. A dense, fresh lawn sloped down to the hazy river; splendid old trees were everywhere; the serious stone house had been built with the simple notions of comfort that existed a hundred years ago.

Mr. Royce, who met him at the station, seemed a peaceful sort of person, too—a man whose forebears had been more like fairy god-parents than ordinary ancestors, for they had given him a handsome, healthy body, a fair fortune, a respected name, and, best of all, an unquestioning belief in all the institutions of his own time, such as matrimony, the ten commandments, and the blessings of paternity.

Despard turned the conversation toward the daughter, but was soon aware that he was getting a mere echo of Mrs. Royce's opinions.

"The child has worked herself into an abnormal frame of mind," said her father.

"You draw this from your own observations?"

"Well, more from her mother's. I leave that sort of thing to my wife. She has great cares, great responsibilities. She takes life almost too seriously." He sighed. The next instant his face lighted up in pointing out to Despard a giant chestnut-tree just saved from a blighting disease. For a few minutes he spoke on the subject with extraordinary vividness.

Despard was quick to recognize expert knowledge, and Royce, with something approaching a blush, admitted that he did understand the care of native trees. "I have sometimes thought of writing a book about it," he said timidly.

"You certainly should."

"Ah, it's so difficult to find time."

Despard smiled. Who had leisure if this favored being had not? He himself, without one hour in the twenty-four that he could call his own, was already at work on his third.

He met the whole family assembled at luncheon: a pale German governess, three little boys, and the dark-eyed Celia, sweet-mouthed but sullen-browed.

Despard, who had had no breakfast, thought more than he would have confessed about the victuals set before him. Any family ought to be amiable, he thought, on food at once so simple and delicious. His opinion of Mrs. Royce rose still higher.

Within the next hour he came to the conclusion that, in spite of his extended knowledge of American interiors, he had never before been in a really well-appointed house—a house, that is, where one wise and affectionate person directed every detail. Mrs. Royce, he found, knew every aspect of her home. She not only knew her flowers almost as individuals, but she knew the vase and the place where each appeared to the best advantage.

She knew better than her husband which chair he liked, where he kept his cigars, and which little table would be best at his elbow. Nor was her consideration confined to her own family. She had thought of a tired doctor's special needs. She had given him "a little room, where he could be quiet and get a glimpse of the river."

Shut in this room, not so very little after all, he walked to the writing-table to make a memorandum. It had more than once happened to him to find, in a house accounted luxurious, only a dry, encrusted inkstand in the spare room. Not so here. Never was ink so fluidly, greenly new; never was blotting-paper so eagerly absorbent. He noticed, besides three sizes of paper and envelopes, that there were cable blanks, telegraph blanks, and postal cards, as well as stamps of all varieties.

It was not Despard's habit to notice life quite as much in detail as this, but now it amused him to pursue the subject. Luxury he knew; but this effective consideration he rated as something higher.

II

HE had arrived on a Friday, and on Sunday at five—things were apt to happen by a schedule in the Royce household—he was to give his report on Celia.

He entered the library—the spot designated by Mrs. Royce—by one door as Churchley, the butler, came in at the other to serve tea.

The dark, shining little table was brought out, noiselessly opened, covered with a cloth—the wrong cloth, Mrs. Royce indicated. Churchley whisked away and returned incredibly quickly with the right one. The tray, weighted with silver and blossoming with the saffron flame of the tea-kettle, was next put before her, and then another little structure of shelves was set at her right hand. Her eye fell on this.

"I said *brown*-bread toast, Churchley." The man murmured and again whisked away.

All this time Despard had not sat down, although between orders Mrs. Royce had more than once urged him to do so. He stood, having shut the door behind him, leaning the point of his shoulder against the wall.

Utterly undisturbed by his calm eyes fixed upon her, Mrs. Royce said:

"Poor Churchley, he has been with us for six years, but I'm afraid I can't keep him. He forgets everything."

"He's on the edge of a nervous breakdown," answered Despard coolly, and he added: "The housemaid is a pronounced neurasthenic. As for your daughter——"

"Ah, Celia, poor, dear child! Must we send her away?" her mother asked, but before the doctor had time to answer, Churchley, by a miracle of celerity, again entered, this time bearing toast of the desired complexion.

After he had finally disappeared, Mrs. Royce busied herself with flame and kettle and tea-caddy before she repeated her question, and her voice had in it a faint sediment of these preoccupations:

"I hope you do not think it necessary to send Celia away, Dr. Despard?"

He drew a chair forward and sat down. "No, Mrs. Royce," he said; "I think it necessary to send you away."

"*Me?*"

He bowed.

"But my health is excellent. Oh, I see," she smiled. "My husband has been talking to you about my responsibilities. Yes, they are great, but one is given strength to do what is required of one. I shall not have to desert my post. I am strong."

"I know you are strong, Mrs. Royce," said he, "but you are the cause of weakness in others. We need not multiply examples: your daughter, the governess, Churchley———"

She broke in—"Of course, I admit their weakness. But don't you see how I protect and support them? How could you imagine that I was the cause?"

"Isn't it suggestive that practically every one with whom you come in contact———"

"My husband," she retorted, quoting an instance against him.

"Your husband has great natural calm, and spends eight hours a day out of the house. You have made this home, this really wonderful home, for those you love. No one admires the achievement more than I do. But you have sacrificed too much of yourself in doing it; and I'm not speaking of your physical strength. In this library, in which you are so fond of sitting, how many books have you ever read?"

"I was a great reader as a girl," she answered.

"Which of these have you read in the last ten years?"

She murmured that he perhaps hardly understood the demands upon her time.

"You never read. You can't," he returned. "Since my first hour here I have been watching you, not your daughter. Her case is simple enough. You don't read, Mrs. Royce, not because you have no time, but because you have no concentration. This is one of the many sacrifices you have made to your household—a serious one, and we must face the results. I have watched you each day carrying the morning papers about with you until evening, and then, if you read the headlines, it is as much as you can accomplish."

She had been staring at him as though in a trance, but now she came to, with a laugh.

"My dear Dr. Despard," she said, "if you were the mother of four children and the head——"

He held up his hand. "You must let me finish," he said. "You have made this home, and you administer it with consummate ability; and yet no one is really happy in it, least of all yourself. Why? Well, I need not remind you that no one is made happy merely by things. Some continuity of inner life is absolutely necessary, not only to happiness but to health. Remember, I am speaking as a nerve specialist. You, Mrs. Royce, are an enemy to continuity. You dispel concentration as a rock dispels a wave. Even I find no little difficulty, when in your presence, in pursuing a consecutive train of thought, and, as for you yourself, such a thing has long been impossible for you. Even now, on this matter so immensely important to you, you have not been able to give me your undivided attention. Other facts have kept coming up in your consciousness—that a bell rang somewhere; that the hearth has not been swept up. Acutely aware as I am of your point of view, these breaks in your attention have been breaks in mine, too; but I have been able to overcome them, and follow my ideas to the end, because I have been trained to do so, and, besides, I've been here only two days. In two days more I would not answer for myself. I should begin to see things, things, things, and to believe that all life was merely a question of arrangements. Even your religion, Mrs. Royce, in which most people find some continuity, is a question of things—of Sunday-schools and altar decoration. That poor little clergyman who lunched here to-day—he came emanating a certain spiritual peace; but he went away crushed by your poor opinion of him as an executive. At this moment he is probably breaking up the current of his life by a conscientious attention to things."

Deeply protesting as she was in her heart, something in his hard, clear look kept her silent, and he went on:

"Your daughter is—to use a big word—an intellectual. For the time being she is interested only in things of the mind. New ideas, books, poetry are the great adventures of life to her at present. To all this you are an obstructionist——"

"There, at least, you are utterly at fault," cried the poor lady, with a passion she had not known for years. "I have done everything in my power to help. I am very ambitious in regard to my children's education. Their schools, their teachers——"

"Ay," said Despard, "you have set out the counters for them but you have never let them play the game. You were interested in making the arrangements, but you had no interest at all in the state of mind which could take advantage of them. Your daughter knows, not only that you take no thought for such matters yourself, but that every phase of your contact with her demands her attention for other matters—clothes, manners, hours, and dates. You have no respect for her preoccupations. Not once, not twice, but fifty times a day, you interrupt her, with a caress, or an errand, or more often a reproof. Yesterday, when she was obviously absorbed in reading that bit of verse to her father, you sent her up-stairs to change her shoes——"

"They were wet; she would have caught cold."

"If you had listened you would have seen she had only four more lines to read. You do all this, not only when she is in your domain, at meals and in the drawing-room, but you follow her to her own room and go in without knocking. I venture to say that that child works at night, for the simple reason that to work in this house during the daytime is impossible."

"Really," said Mrs. Royce, "with the best will in the world I do not understand you. Celia's friends sometimes seem to feel that I ought to neglect her manners and pronunciation, ought to allow her to become selfish and self-centred, so that she may—" She broke off as if words failed her. "But I have never heard a grown person suggest that such a course would be right."

"Ask your clergyman what is right," answered Despard. "I am here to tell you what is healthy; I am here to prescribe. Now, notice, please, I do not tell you to change. I don't think you could. The reactions have taken place too many times. I tell you to go away. We can call it a rest cure. You shall have beautiful surroundings, comfort, and, above all that leisure that recent years have failed to give you. In return I shall ask you to concentrate your mind for a certain number of hours each day."

"You talk," she cried bitterly, "as if I enjoyed the treadmill of my daily life."

"You have unusual executive ability, and most of us enjoy the use of our powers."

"The best refutation of all that you have said is that I am eager to go," she returned. "Ah, I cannot tell you how inviting such a prospect seems to me—not to order dinner, not to have to decide and arrange for every one, not to be the pivot of the whole structure. Ah, Dr. Despard, I would so gladly go, but——"

"But?"

"But what would happen to my family without me?"

"They must try looking out for themselves," he answered. He glanced at his watch, for he was to take a train that afternoon; and Mrs. Royce collected herself enough to touch the bell—it always hung within tempting reach of her hand—and gave Churchley orders to send for the motor and have the doctor's bags brought down.

During this interval Despard walked to the window and stood looking out. It is not always so easy to apply the knife psychologically as physically. He wondered if he could have been more gentle and equally effective. As he stood there Celia came sauntering across the lawn, her head bent, her hands deep in the pockets of an enveloping dun-colored coat. The brow which had first seemed sulky to him appeared now simply thoughtful.

III

THE strength of Mrs. Royce's character was shown by the fact that she obeyed—she actually went. She went almost gladly— a state of mind induced by the extraordinary activity of her last days at home. In one brilliant flash of prophecy and power she foresaw and forestalled every contingency that could arise in her absence. She departed in a condition of exhaustion fully justifying the doctor's story of a needed rest.

Her weariness lasted through the first few days at the sanatorium. She was well content to lie in bed and think of nothing. But by the fifth or sixth day she began to wonder where she had left the key of the cedar closet; and several possibilities of error in the arrangements she had made to reach from garret to cellar began to creep into her consciousness. Her elder boy was subject to throat trouble; her younger was subtly averse to bathing. She had not, perhaps, sufficiently emphasized these two dangers. She had, however, given her promise not to communicate with her household except in case of necessity.

Conscientious in her determination to do what she had set out to do, she took out some of the books she had brought with her, but they seemed an unsatisfactory lot: the novels, trashy; the essays, dull; the history, heavy. Strange, she thought, how people will recommend books which really did not even hold one's attention.

The word attention, bringing with it the recollection of Despard's speech, recalled her to her obligations. Heavy or not, she was resolved to make her way through the volume.

She read: "It has been argued that the too rapid introduction of modern political machinery, and the too rapid unification of such different populations as those—" Had she told them not to keep the house too hot in these first spring days? Overheated houses, in her opinion, were a fruitful source of ill health. "—though these may with more justice be ascribed to deep-seated sociological causes stretching back through two thousand years—" This was the season for putting away the furs. If, in her absence, moths should attack her husband's sable-lined overcoat! Ah, she put down her book; this was serious.

Fifteen minutes later she went out, trying to walk off the haunting presence of that fur coat.

There was something not a little heroic in her struggle with temptations—staying on while every notion she had heretofore considered righteous called to her to go back. Hideous pictures of ruin and discomfort at home floated before her mind. She had to admit she found a certain grim satisfaction in such visions. They would at least prove to Despard how little the modern family is able to dispense with the services of the old-fashioned mother.

She was human enough to be eager to prove him wrong in essentials, for in minor matters he had shown himself terribly accurate. With unlimited leisure on her hands she was surprised to find how little enjoyment she derived from her books. She read herself to sleep with a novel every night, but it was enough for her to open one of the more serious works for her mind to rush back to the old domestic problems. Her eyes alone would read the printed page.

Her life seemed hideously vacant—empty, as she put it, of all affection; but it was also empty of all machinery—perhaps the greater change of the two. She had no small duties, no orders to give, no mistakes to correct.

She was not forbidden to communicate with Despard, and at the end of a week she telegraphed him that she was going home. He came to her at once.

"I am doing what I know to be wrong," she broke out. "I am neglecting my family."

"You are doing what your medical adviser orders."

"Yes," she answered, "but can you guarantee that nothing will happen in my absence? Will it be any comfort to me, if things go wrong, to say that I was obeying orders?"

He did not directly answer this question, which had been largely rhetorical in intention. Instead, he said:

"Yes, I suppose you are dreadfully bored."

She checked an impulse toward complete denial. He had stated half the truth. She was bored, but she tried to make him see that there was more than that in her attitude. He, a man and a bachelor, could hardly realize how serious might be the results of a mother's protracted absence.

He had at times a trick—irritating to Mrs. Royce—of replying to something slightly different from the thought one had expressed. He did so now.

"And if they do miss you," he said, "won't that be a help?"

Yes, certainly, it would be a help, and it was perhaps that thought which kept her on day after day—the thought that they were missing her in every detail of life, the belief that the daily service, the common-place sacrifice of an existence like hers could only be realized by its cessation.

One reward she had. Her books began to grow more interesting. "It grows better as you get into it," she explained to one of the nurses, but in her heart she knew the improvement was not in the book.

At last a night came when she had a dream, more poignant, more vivid than any material message could have been—a dream of disaster at home. She was not a superstitious woman, but the impression already in her mind was immensely deepened. She was needed at home; that was her place. What madness it had been for her to go away, and what a selfish madness, made up partly of desire to rest and partly of a wish to prove Despard wrong! She might have cause to reproach herself for the remainder of her life. She could forgive him all that she herself had suffered, removed from her work, deprived of all occupation and happy home activities, but if anything had gone wrong with those she loved——

That very afternoon she went home.

Once inside her own gates she began to see signs of her three weeks' absence. Although the grounds were nominally her husband's charge, the standards since her departure had evidently been lowered. The gutters were but half cleared and the gravel unraked. The appearance of the house confirmed her fears. The window curtains had not been changed. Sixty-two dirty window curtains seemed to her to offer but a dreary welcome.

In spite of sunshine, the rainy-day door mat greeted her, left from the day before, which had been rainy; and the brasses of the door, though not actually tarnished, lacked that elysian brightness on which she herself insisted.

As she mounted the steps two of the boys came running up—hugging and clawing at her with hands on which she caught a glimpse of the lustrous veneer of dirt. They were so glad to see her; and little Lewis had been ill. Her heart stood still—oh, only a cold. Where was he? she asked them, and when they said—oh, horror!—out with the governess in the pony cart, she sent them racing after him.

The darkest forebodings filled her mind as to what she would find within. She rang and, after an interval too long by several minutes, Churchley opened the door. For an instant his appearance drove all other thoughts away.

"Why, Churchley," she cried, "you have been putting on weight!"

Churchley acknowledged the imputation with a smile that approached dangerously near a dimple.

"Yes, madame," he said, "I've taken a great turn for the better," and he asked sympathetically after her own health.

She made no answer, but, turning her head away from the staircase, in whose crevices she had already detected faint gray lines of dust, she moved toward the library door, which Churchley quietly opened for her.

She saw with a shock that the arrangement of the furniture— an arrangement sanctified by twenty years of habit—had been altered. Two desks had been drawn near the windows without any respect for symmetry, and at these, back to back, her husband and daughter were sitting.

That Celia should bring her school-books to the library, though unusual, was not unnatural, but the sight of Royce at work on page after page of foolscap was something requiring an explanation.

The room was perfectly quiet except for the scratch of his pen and the ticking of the clock; and Mrs. Royce decided that she would stand there silent until some other interruption occurred. It could not be very long before a servant entered or they themselves would weary of this work.

But the silence continued. Once Royce took out a book and glanced at some reference. Once Celia got up and lighted the lamps for both, but neither of them spoke.

For a long time Mrs. Royce stood there, transfixed by a curious conviction that came to her as she watched—the conviction that this silence carried with it a more perfect companionship than all her long talks with her husband had ever brought. Of course, she had long since realized that, as gradually as one season melts into another, her relationship to her husband had changed—changed inevitably, she had imagined, from the poetry of first love into something that resembled the prose of a business partnership. To her the change was not altogether to be regretted; in her eyes the business of being the head of a man's house and the mother of his children was still charged with the romantic idea. But for the first time it now occurred to her to ask whether the change had been equally satisfactory to him. Ah, she admitted that a certain charm, a certain stimulation had gone from their affection, but never before had she thought, as she was thinking now, that the quality most conspicuously absent was intimacy. How was such a thing possible when she had lived twenty years of her life with him in perfect amity?

Yet, standing there, she saw that for many years she had not had the least conception of what had been going on in his mind. She had used the word business partnership, and, naturally, when they were together they often discussed the details of the business, only now she remembered that it was always in *her* department that the problems for discussion arose. Royce seemed to be able to manage his end of it without consultation. Why was this?

She tried desperately to see the thing clearly. Her whole life was built on the belief that she existed solely to be depended upon; and yet she saw that her husband, in all his more personal interests, far from depending on her, never even mentioned them to her. What did that mean? And why had she never observed this contradiction before? Could it be that, after all, she was not dependable, or had some unreckoned factor in his life rendered Royce more self-reliant than he had been in the early days of their marriage?

And at this point, before she realized her intention, she heard her own voice saying: "Celia, my dear, your lamp is flaring."

Well, there was no question of the welcome with which both pairs of eyes lit up. "Mother, *dear!*" cried the girl. Both overwhelmed her with solicitude about her health. She did not have to ask after theirs. Never were two rosier, more unlined faces than theirs.

After a moment she asked what it was that her husband was writing, and he answered, almost timidly, that it was a book on trees; he had had the idea in his mind for a number of years but had never had the energy to begin it before.

"Why not?" she asked almost sharply, but before he had time to answer—and it was evident he himself had no idea of the real answer—Celia broke in:

"And what do you think, mother? I've won the prize for composition at school. I had the idea the very night you went away, and I've worked and worked over it, and they all say that it is much better than anything I ever did before. Aren't you glad?"

Yes, her mother was glad, but a strain of bitterness mingled with her rejoicing. Was it, indeed, her absence that had released all the vital energy?

One hope lingered unacknowledged in her breast. She turned to her husband.

"And have they made you comfortable since I went?" she asked.

"Oh, perfectly," he replied. "Everything has gone without a hitch, thanks to your arrangements."

"Yes," Celia chimed in, "the servants have been too wonderful; they've done everything just as if you were at home, only better."

Mrs. Royce looked round the room, where to her eye everything was wrong—the corners dusty, the lamps ill-cared for, the sofa pillows rumpled, and the tea-tray, which ought to have been removed, still standing disordered in a corner.

She stretched her hand toward the bell to ring and order it taken away; and then, checking herself, she sank back and folded her hands idly in her lap. Her husband had begun to tell her something about his book.

www.ingramcontent.com/pod-product-compliance
Lightning Source LLC
LaVergne TN
LVHW091238080426
835509LV00009B/1327